Yellow Hippo

by
Alan Rogers

for
Charlotte

TWO CAN ™

PRINCETON ■ LONDON

Yellow Hippo has a yellow cart.

She takes it for a walk.

Yellow Hippo has a yellow guitar . . .

to put on her yellow cart.

Yellow Hippo has a yellow melon . . .

to put on her yellow cart.

Yellow Hippo has a yellow coat . . .

to put on her yellow cart.

Yellow Hippo has a yellow hat . . .

to put on her yellow cart.

Yellow Hippo has a yellow umbrella . . .

and it looks like rain.

Yellow Hippo hurries home . . .

and doesn't see the yellow ladder . . .

SPLAT!